ALLIE'S MOVIE ADVENTURE

Allie's Adventures Series
written by
DEBORAH SMITH FORD

Kindle Direct Publishing (KDP)

Copyright © 2021 by Deborah Smith Ford

ISBN 979-8-69-8863397

In Loving Memory
Anna 2005-2020 & Rusty 2006-2019

We say goodbye to our dear canine family members who are part of "Allie's Movie Adventure." They were Rusty Brown and Roly Poly Anna Ford. The two portray canine characters in this sixth of Allie's adventures.

Anna was part Chow and Collie. Rusty Brown was part Hound and Irish Setter. He was a rescue or cell dog trained by an inmate at a correctional center. Later he was welcomed into Chuck and Becky Brown's home.

Rusty and Anna were not in movies nor on TV shows, but they were clever, playful, and protective. Anna was featured in the fifth book of *Allie's Adventures Series*.

Rusty was born and raised in Florida. Anna was born in Mississippi and pudgy at birth. She traveled as a pup with two of her seven siblings to Florida where she lived out her life.

Rusty and Anna's families and friends remember their mischievous ways, guarding their homes, and unconditional love. Enjoy images of them at "Allie's Movie Memories" in center of book. Anna and Rusty, you are missed.

Acknowledgements

With multiple skills required in writing a book, more went into "Allie's Movie Adventure" than one could imagine. I could not have done it without the help of every single one of you.
Thank you!

Book Details
Courtney Baldwin, DVM - support & formatting
Alana Joos - foreword
Janna Joos – editing

Photo, Poem & Art Submissions
AOK Pictures - photos
Kristin Mercedes Bence - photos
Dr. Klara Boryskova - cover & inside photos
Becky Brown - inspiration & photo
Calder - poem & art
Cora as Allie - inspiration & photos
Captain Carl "Fizz" Fismer - photos
Roger Kabler - art
Doreen Lehner - photos
Peter Noone - photo
Marlene Palumbo of Indienink Music - photos
Heather, Hadley & Ivy Steht - photos

Author's Note

This work of fiction is based on real lives and events. It is not necessarily 100% factual. It is meant to be enjoyed!

Adventures happen in any location, and Allie's favorites include islands and seashores. This book's cover was inspired by an original photo taken by Dr. Klara Boryskova. She shot it in French Polynesia in the South Pacific Ocean.

Main character Allie's original adventure was not on an island. Rather, it was on "The Little Apple" farm. Her adventures grew into *Allie's Adventures Book Series*.

Memories later used in Allie's adventures began in the 1950s, taking shape by 1985. My first book was published in 2009, with more to follow.

These stories, for the young and the young at heart, are seen through Allie's eyes. She and friends explore beaches, mansions, film sets, and more!

Allie's recent adventure is about working on a movie set. Erik Krefeld wrote and produced the film after being inspired by the book of the same name, *Love Song & Power (LSP)* by Stevie Kinchen. The film and LSP book are suited for a mature audience, but producing the film remains the same.

Experiencing 25 years in showbiz serves as most of this book's research. Working on *LSP* was rewarding and helped influence the theme of "Allie's Movie Adventure."

A pandemic caused a longer filming time frame, from 2019-2020. The film's release date is 2021.

"The shooting of a movie can be magical. After the movie is wrapped, edited, and promoted the real magic begins!" - Allie

Deborah Smith Ford, AlliesAdventures.com

Contents

Foreword

Deborah Smith Ford's creative storytelling takes us on another adventure with Allie. She is a young girl who grew up on an apple farm. Her passion for travel, exploring, and new experiences allows her to embrace the excitement and curiosity of life as expressed in *Allie's Adventures Book Series.*

"Allie's Movie Adventure" takes us on a movie set where Allie enjoys the spotlight and is surrounded by talented and creative people. This book offers a behind the scenes tour of shooting a movie with explanations of terms and phrases used in the world of entertainment.

I have had the distinct pleasure of working with Deborah. We have worked together on many events including The Reel Awards, and her skills as an actress and author are commendable!

Alana Joos
Professional Drummer & Entertainment Producer

Chapter 1
Dream Studios

My family drives me to a movie set where I will be part of its cast and crew. The door leading to that adventure is found at Dream Studios (DS).

Duncan "Dunky" owns DS, and he lives next to it. On the land behind DS complex is a barn and livestock. That reminds me of our apple farm and past summer vacations on our family farms.

A constant at Dunky's side are two canine companions, Anna and Rusty. Additional "pets" include Sparkles, his horse, and chickens that scratch and roam. Film producer Erik says all the farm critters will be in the film!

On our apple farm we had one pet; he was a Boxer dog named Baron. The farm had no livestock, just apples. Dunky, with friend Rita, must keep busy with the farm and studios.

My friends mean a lot to me. One of them is Prana. Her first name is pronounced with two short a's. Songbird is her last name, and it matches her beautiful voice.

Being a bit nervous working on a movie set finds myself twisting two fingers around my red messenger bag's straps. Mom sees this and shares.

"Allie," Mom calmly says, "in our lives sometimes one's lucky enough to have one friend who is wise and who we trust; you have two."

"They are Miss Becky and Prana, right?!" Allie quickly shouts, "When we met, there was a connection. They are talented too. Prana loves her family, and she entertains on stage, records CDs, creates educational videos, and has been cast in lead film roles. Her husband Erik is her manager."

Mom says, "I didn't know all that about her."

"Miss Becky," Allie says, "is an actress, model, film wardrobe supervisor, local volunteer, and former beauty queen. Most of all, she is a loving wife, mother, and grandmother or 'gramacita.'"

Mom says, "Allie, you feel better now?"

Mom can be tricky like that. It worked. I do feel better.

Allie says, "Thanks Mom."

Giving me permission to work on this project shows how much my parents think of the film and those behind it. Erik, with AOK Pictures, is the creator of this film, and he was influenced by Stevie Kinchen's book of the same name.

Getting up early, earlier than for school, is required to work on most films. My parents drop me off soon, and the sun has not even shown its face.

Prana, Miss Becky, Ivy, and others will be my guardians when on and off the movie set. Erik told my parents that they can visit on set any time they want. Mom and Dad will receive text updates on the film's shooting locations. Film scenes will be shot at different places, both interior and exterior.

Soundstages are used for shooting films, and that is one reason Dream Studios was chosen. This building houses three studios making photography, green screening, and recording available to musicians and film companies.

Violet is Prana's film character. Both the fictious and real women portray professional singers. I will sing too.

Prana's coaching should improve my vocals, then Erik will record us singing. The two of us will use a vocal booth, but first we will rehearse. Rehearsals are a good idea!

Hearing my stomach growl, Mom reminds me that Erik is cooking breakfast this morning. My folks drop me off and leave. I hear the driveway's gravel crunch under Dad's tires.

Suddenly a sack of chicken feed, with legs, runs up to me. About to collide, I yell out.

Allie screams, "Watch out!"

Dropping the sack, he apologizes. Picking up the sack, he runs again; chickens follow.

Before opening the back door an aroma of bacon and eggs fills the air. It is easy to smell, and see, that breakfast is ready. Handsomely seated on a blue platter are toasted bagels and cream cheese comfortably nestled up against eggs and bacon. Dunky's chickens probably donated the eggs.

A red bowl of fresh cut fruit proudly sits on the table. Orange juice and milk are offered on the counter. I choose juice. There will be room for hot cocoa later!

"Listen to me! I'm the PRODUCER!" is painted on the front of Erik's apron. He pulls up stools.

Erik says, "You just missed Dunky."

So that was him!

My mind is elsewhere, as I fill up my plate. On leashes, Dunky's Anna and Rusty greeted me from afar. It was dark outside, but one could still tell the size of the pups, big!

Prana says grace before pouring juice and joining us. I ask her to remind me why she avoids dairy products.

Prana says, "Sorry, this is gross, especially at the table, but my good friend and voice coach, Carla, advises me against eating or drinking dairy products and other fatty foods 1-2 hours before singing. Extra mucus is produced, and that 'attacks' the vocal cords.

"The result is temporary, but it causes havoc to a singer's voice at inappropriate times – like performing on stage or when filming! Whispering can hurt throats too, causing permanent damage. Carla describes it better. No matter what, I listen to Carla!"

"Thanks." says Allie, "Yes, mucus is gross but important to know. No more whispering either; I'm putting both of those tips in my journal!"

Prana has sung and acted professionally over a decade. In the film she will use both her singing and acting abilities.

The crunching of bacon does not distract from hearing a familiar voice. It is Miss Becky's!

"Good morning, Prana and Allie!" Miss Becky shouts, "Sorry to interrupt, but Prana tells me, Allie, that you two will be singing together!"

Prana, "That's for sure!"

Miss Becky continues, "For that reason both of you need something special to wear. Erik brought on a fashion designer who is a friend of mine. His name is Victor "Vic" Miller of Victor Miller Designs. I will measure you. He already measured Prana. In the film she will be wearing one or more of his amazing designs. In my scenes I will wear a design by Victor Miller too. I am not sure what he'll create for you."

It is good seeing Miss Becky, and I am excited to hear about the fashion designer. She needs help after breakfast and reminds me to bring my script. My set bag remains across my chest ready to go.

After thanking Erik for breakfast, I offer to tidy up. He turns me down saying other than the frying pan, everything is disposable.

"Thanks though." Erik says, "I try not to use paper and plastic, but this is an exception. By the way, in case you have not seen the call sheet, our script supervisor is Deb. She is the same Deb from last year at the Sunburst Convention. You will be working with her, and your title is script girl. Allie, I'm happy that you're part of the team!"

Erik is off in a flash.

Before leaving the table, Prana gives me a hug. It is our own "feel good hug."

One of the two largest studios of the complex is off the kitchen. The voice heard inside the first studio belongs to Miss Becky. As I venture in to find her, I can hardly believe my eyes. Our house is big, but DS is bigger, and it has everything needed to shoot a film. This building is the main location for shooting *Love Song and Power*. Dream Studios is our home away from home.

Chapter 2

Call Sheet

The film's entire cast and crew, including myself, have worked for several days. Christian gives Dunky's guests a tour. He points to double doors describing them as the loading and unloading docks.

Deb yells, "Take ten!"

This is the perfect time to venture outside. Like everyone else, we have only seen the property coming and going in the dark. What a treat to see it now in daylight. Grabbing an apple and camera I head out.

Past the loading dock to the front is a white picket fence. From there, wire-like fencing wraps around to the back. High fences help keep pets and livestock safe.

Dunky walks by and asks if I would like a tour.

Allie, "Yes thanks, but not a long one."

Dunky holds my camera to make eating an apple easier. We head toward the barn.

"This farm is small." says Dunky, "It only has one horse, several chickens and two dogs."

Allie laughs, "That is more critters than were on our apple farm unless you count the wildlife. Deer, squirrels, birds, and a stray cat visited us."

We return to Dream Studios' back door.

Dunky says, "This complex has everything entertainment professionals need. It houses three large studios labeled A, B and C, real original, right? Other areas include a small kitchen and living room; together they are called the green room. We can't forget the bathroom off the hallway."

Inside, Dunky points to walls hosting posters of famous musicians. He tells me that the studios' "Entertainers Hall of Fame" includes Shaw Davis & The Black Ties, Bridget Kelly and Tim Fik of The Bridget Kelly Band, Rob Whitehurst, Peter Noone, and more!

Dunky says, "Allie, you or your family may know of the famous English pop and rock group, Herman's Hermits. The band formed in 1964. Peter Noone, aka Herman, was and maybe still is the band's lead singer. Either way, Noone continues to perform their 60's music. The 'guys' and I have one thing in common; we're from England!"

We walk back inside, and Dunky says he is confident that our film's poster will be on the wall soon. I agree.

"Allie," Dunky shares, "You may see musicians coming and going. Having soundproof walls, anyone can record and shoot at the same time."

Dunky gives me my camera, winks, walks away, and my break is over.

Allie shouts out, "Thanks Dunky!"

Around the corner Miss Becky and Prana are busy. Miss Becky sees me and says the schedule changed again, ten more minutes.

Allie yells, "Miss Becky, going outside! Will return in another ten, please tell Deb if you see her, thanks!"

Back outside Miss Becky is on my mind. After she won a beauty queen title, she traveled all over the world representing pageants… once a beauty queen, always a beauty queen. Miss Becky is beautiful on the inside as well. She and hubby Chuck keep in touch with us, and our families visit each other's homes.

When my friends and I worked behind the stages at The Reel Awards and Sunburst Convention, being quiet was a necessity. Movie sets require the same kind of quiet.

Sparkles sees me taking photos of the chickens, and she comes running. Sparkles loves attention. She runs away, turns around, runs back, and stops quickly at the fence line throwing her head back. What a great shot!

At my feet, the chickens cluck and peck acting as if they are hungry. Chickens are always hungry!

Time to return to work. Miss Becky greets me.

She says, "Welcome back. You are needed on set. Tell me later about your escapades."

Deb, on set, is near the camera's monitor, and she has saved me a seat. Being close we can see the scenes' details.

The film's line producer is Heather. She stands nearby ready for anything. She, Ivy, and Hadley are family. They drove here from out of state, and the three of them work hard.

Heather has many film responsibilities, and one of them is creating call sheets. Everyone gets a call sheet for each shoot day. The sheet has names of all the cast and crew, their contact info, call times, the weather, that day's location, and the closest hospital.

In a corner, Archer and Hadley are on the floor coloring. Some of what they color is "Ivy's Art." Ivy is an amazing sketch artist, and she draws for the kids. Ivy is "in charge" of the three of us as well, and that is a good thing. Ivy is neato!

Changing locations calls for film crew to load and unload vehicles and set up and break down their stations. For obvious reasons it is nice staying at one place for a while.

After many takes the actors get a break. During this quiet time Deb and I review the call sheet and script.

Patience is needed when making a movie. Shooting and editing take a long time; they can take months.

Deb and I stay close to the camera. This scene's director of photography (DP) is Eddel. He and Erik are co-directors.

Shooting should end, or wrap, soon. It will be close to the time school begins. Deb clears her throat, back to real life. We continue shooting.

Chapter 3
Love, Song & Prana

Feeling homesick comes easily to me, and Prana knows that. She keeps a watchful eye.

It will not be long until we are wrapped. When shooting ends, post-production begins. We enjoy each moment.

Work will continue for Erik, but he knows that. Editor is another of his hats. Editing is crucial, but this is not Erik's first rodeo!

Before the film screens, everyone is contacted in time to attend. At these screenings, the cast and crew will enjoy seeing what they have created. Usually, films are shown on a big silver screen. Everyone hopes that the film is nominated and/or wins awards; then we walk down The Red Carpet!

Prana calls for me. Another daydream is dashed. That is okay. Work comes first, happy to be needed. Deb says I am free to leave, and Heather can fill in if needed. Since we work together well, most of us can switch hats when necessary.

"Allie, you're fast." says Prana, "Miss Becky needs help. Some clothes have been hung up, but more just arrived. Since organizing is one of your skills, you are the chosen one for this assignment. You will need your script. I bet you already know that. Thanks!"

Prana looks at the clock. She knows she is to be back on set soon.

Ivy assists Prana in makeup. Miss Becky checks Prana's wardrobe and accessories. My organizing new clothing frees up Miss Becky. There are few clothes; it will not take long.

Prana gets dressed and approved by Miss Becky. Ivy, with her makeup kit, follows Prana onto set. For me, it is back to work too, my other work. Miss Becky stays behind steaming an actor's shirt and yells out to me, "Thanks Allie!"

We shoot part of the scene. For a break, most of the cast visit craft services and the green room. Some of them have wardrobe-related questions. Miss Becky has little downtime.

Taking a break with Prana finds me walking at a fast clip. She is hard to keep up with, and anyone can tell she is on a mission. Dunky is up ahead. He nods, as we pass each other. Prana says he is always busy. She should talk!

Turns out Prana is searching for her sheet music. She finds it, and with papers in hand heads to the wardrobe station where Miss Becky is waiting.

Passing craft services, we grab bottles of water. When the noisy air conditioning is turned off, like now, water is needed more than ever. With vehicles outside moving on gravel and airplanes overhead, we cannot open windows.

Before going back on set Prana puts the papers away in a safe place, in her tote bag. The sheet music is important, and we will both be using it later.

Miss Becky makes certain Prana's clothes are perfect. Ivy freshens her makeup, and Prana takes off to set!

What is that on the floor? It is an earring. It is Prana's! This script girl, with earring in hand, runs after Prana. However, she is already on set in front of the camera. Not thinking, I yell "Cut!" Everyone stops. After handing her the earring, I return to my script girl seat. There's silence, followed by smiles.

As a bad joke an unknown gruff voice says, "That's not her earring."

Prana gives the culprit "a look" and says, "Yes, it is. Thanks Allie!"

"Whew!" says Eddel, "Back to one!"

That means we start from where we left off. The scene is shot and wrapped. We take another break, as they get ready for the next scene. Looking around I try guessing who the culprit might have been. Prana will tell me later.

Back in the set-up room, next to the piano on the floor, is a black bag. Each crew member is responsible for his or her department's equipment. Deb usually checks on me, but this time it is the other way around. Her bag is black. A closer look reveals that the bag by the piano is NOT Deb's, good, will leave it alone.

A script person's "equipment" consists of one bag of necessities. The two of us each have a bag that contains a notebook with script, paper, call sheet, stopwatch, pencil, plus a sharpener and eraser. We have a pen, but since it is difficult erasing ink it is used for other purposes. We seldom need a stopwatch; if we do, that is Deb's department.

In a few, it will be time to return to set. The black bag that was by the piano is already gone. Ha! There's Erik with it on his shoulder.

Leaning against the wall at the end of the hallway is a good place to be. At this spot I can see and hear both Deb and Miss Becky at the same time. The bathroom and craft services are close by too!

When I ask Miss Becky about her organizing skills, she says she has been told that "organized" is her middle name, meaning she always is. She arranges clothes in such a way that anyone can go to a rack and grab what is needed. She prefers doing the grabbing though.

Miss Becky keeps a smaller rack handy for previously used clothes on sets. Later they are checked for defects and wrinkles, then rehung. That reminds me of libraries; only a librarian returns books to shelves!

Miss Becky checks wardrobe photos often to confirm that outfits are perfect. She usually retrieves those details from her head!

Prana sounds upset, "I can't find my sides! May I borrow yours Allie?!"

Handing Prana my script is a good move. However, she returns mine soon, as hers is found hiding between the wall and her handbag. Sides is the nickname for a script. An owner of a script tends to write on its sides. Their own copy is important and unique. With her sides in hand, Prana is ecstatic.

"Yay!" Prana yells, "Thanks Allie!"

"Not a problem." Allie responds, "How about if this film has another name?"

Prana asks, "What's that?"

Allie answers, *"Love, Song & Prana"*

Prana gives me one of her special hugs.

Deb is calling. We both run!

Chapter 4

Cast, Crew & Musicians

Next, visiting craft services is a good idea, and those little bottled waters are an even better idea. Peanut butter crackers look good too. The package slides down easily into my bag for a snack later, but not on set.

Chewing gum is not allowed on or off set, and that's why craft services never has it. Smacking sounds and popped bubbles would alert the soundman. Besides, used gum can cause issues too. Drinks with screw on caps are the only thing allowed.

Time flies, and now it is lunchtime. The crew eats, then the talent. Crew always eats first, so they can set up the next scene.

Mealtimes are a challenge to the wardrobe and script supervisors. It is then that actors have accidents. Food spots on their clothes can be seen on film. Spots or stains can happen if an actor fails to use a cover-up. Large towels are often used as cover-ups. Miss Becky tells actors to protect their clothing, but sometimes they forget. It can be a problem if there is no duplicate outfit to replace a stained one. So far, we have been lucky.

Sure enough, there is an actor eating a hamburger with ketchup oozing out the back side. Ahhhhh!

Running to the actor, with a paper towel in hand, the blob of ketchup is caught in the nick of time. With mouth full, the actor cracks half a smile and tries to thank me.

Allie, "You're welcome."

That same actor comes up to me later.

Actor says, "Sorry, I meant to use a cover-up. I will next time. Thanks again. What is your name, and what do you do?"

"I'm Allie. Thanks for understanding." says Allie, "Script girl is my title. See you back on set."

Various cast members come and go. Once they wrap, they are excused. People not needed on set anymore should not be on it!

There are exceptions. Some of them are Mom and Dad, Erik's guests, and invited media. Two of the guests are Dunky and Rita. The film's unit publicist is another one of those guests; she is Marlene Palumbo with Indienink Music. She represents the singers and musicians in this film. Prana, of course, is one of them!

Bridget and Tim Fik of the Bridget Kelly Band and Shaw Davis & The Black Ties band are represented by Marlene as well. She and the band members were here this morning. Marlene watched as each band rehearsed in the chamber room. Bridget sings in the film!

Musicians, and cast and crew work well together; as a result, all runs smoothly. Heather likes things running smoothly.

The men in Heather's family have helped in the past on movie sets. Her husband Robert works back home, and son Robbie is in the military. Her daughter Ivy joined the reserves. Youngest daughter Hadley is younger than me, but she helps with Archer. He is the son of Erik and Prana.

The nice weather is welcoming, so Hadley and Archer play outside. It is hard for Ivy to be in more than one place at a time, so others fill in. Dunky and Rita take turns watching the kids. Rita and Rusty are outside with them now.

Besides watching the kids, Ivy is makeup supervisor, still photographer, and drives. She applies makeup professionally, and the military trained her to drive heavy equipment transport. Those jobs seem opposites!

Ivy transports the non-local film talent to and from their "flats" and film locations. Most likely they have flown here and do not have a car. There is a senior on set who helps, has a car, but she cannot drive in the dark. Ivy helps her too.

Ivy's dad works for a state's department of natural resources as a game warden pilot. This kind of airplane or helicopter pilot assists in the enforcement of state laws for the conservation of wildlife and the protection of fish and game. His flying skills have been used to shoot film scenes too. Being a pilot comes in handy and is helpful.

Robert learned to fly when working in law enforcement. He has been training for a new job. It will be his first civilian job and non-police job working as a pilot for Emergency Medical Services (EMS). He will work as an EMS pilots transport people from accident scenes to medical facilities and from hospital to hospital. His work is important, plus he is a great husband and father!

If today runs long, Ivy will drive Hadley, myself, and Archer to the location that Erik reserved. There we will eat and go to bed early in time to get up and head to set. Film crew work long hours. Our leaving early today sounds good to me. It pays being a kid!

Erik, "Bye! See you tomorrow!"

Erik hugs us goodnight, takes a bite out of an apple and runs back to set. I see Miss Becky and Prana deciding on the next outfit. They wave to us as we go out the door.

When we head to the car, we see Sparkles. She is running toward us on the other side of the fence "talking" as she runs. We head over to her with Ivy and take photos. Sparkles grins saying "cheese!"

A light rain turns into a storm. We run, waving goodbye to Sparkles. She whinnies, turns away, and gallops to the barn. We jump into the car. Towels await us on the back seat. Like her mom, Ivy thinks of everything!

Chapter 5

B-Roll

Sleep came quickly for me last night, but I heard later that Ivy had to comfort Archer. His parents worked late. He missed them. Everyone finally fell asleep.

Waking up excited reminds me of my first day on set. Except now I know what to do!

Last summer cousin Mattie trained me as junior stage manager. At night I stayed with her family either in their home or at the convention center's hotel.

We are back at Dream Studios. Sometimes we work at different locations, but it is good being back at our "work home."

Crew members take camera equipment nearby to get B-Roll footage. Christian is one crew member who shoots some of the B-Roll. He is normally funny all the time, but he is careful and serious using cameras, any camera. Besides, cameras are expensive!

During a serious moment Christian describes B-Roll. He says that it is additional footage that enriches stories adding dimension to a film.

"Whoa," shocked Allie tells him, "Christian, no offense, but you sound like an encyclopedia. Everyone must agree that they don't see that one coming!"

Christian agrees while chuckling. It is hard for him to remain serious. He can be funny and professional at the same time; that is a gift.

Now, many of the interior and exterior shots are wrapped here at DS. Crew has remained the same since day one. We know each other's names. The cast has two names, and I know both. If cast and crew were not already friends/framily, we are now!

Usually, the background actors are not known as well, because they are not on set much. Those actors seldom have a character name and not many, if any, have lines. Film credits for them show up as Waiter, Nurse, Teacher, and so on. Extras, as they are sometimes called, are not usually trained in acting, but some are.

Extras who are serious, study, get a headshot, an agent, and experience. Then they have a good foundation at becoming professional actors making it easier getting cast for featured, supporting, or principal roles. When actors qualify as a union member, they make the decision of joining or not. By the way, all of this does not happen overnight!

For years, Deb worked as crew and as an extra. After studying stage, TV and film acting, getting agents, and working on sets, Deb became union eligible. She had a plan, and she stuck to it, but she still enjoys working behind the scenes. Yes, what Deb shared is in my journal.

There is stage or theatrical acting too, but it is a different cup of tea. A thespian or stage actor requires intense passion. That does not mean film actors are not passionate. Maybe it is a different kind of passion? Either way, it takes perseverance to act, especially if it is your livelihood - acting for a living.

Sometimes cast and crew wear many hats. That means they are responsible for more than one film-related task. Miss Becky, Ivy, Erik, and others are examples of wearing more than one hat. In Miss Becky's case, she is the wardrobe supervisor, and she has an important film role.

It has been a long day, and it is not over. I see Heather giving Ivy instructions. Next, Ivy transports us back to our flat to sleep. We will eat on the way. Our flats or homes are not always the same every night, but they are most of the time. It is better if they are closer to the shoot locations.

Heather and daughters are three needing a place to rest their heads. Sometimes local people, even cast and crew, offer their homes for us to stay; Deb and Miss Becky have.

We return "home" and get ready for bed, going straight to sleep. Ivy is our alarm clock.

Chapter 6
Movie Madness

Ivy whispers, "It's time to get up Allie."

Hadley and Archer, having gotten up early and dressed, crunch and slurp on toast, cereal, milk, and grapes. Dressing quickly will leave more time to eat, oops, not for me!

It is time to go. My teeth sink into an apple on the way out the door. Craft services should have bagels and orange juice. Maybe there will be fruit, hot cocoa too!

While running to the car, my bag hangs on for dear life. I jump in the front seat, as the kids are too small to sit up here. We are off!

It is normal in the movie industry to hurry up and wait. All this rushing is not uncommon when working on film sets. Cast and crew call it movie madness.

For us call time is 8:00 a.m., not sunrise like everyone else. The crew will already be set up. Odds are most wrapped late last night. It is less sleep for them, but that's life on a movie set!

Outside scenes are scheduled, so Heather has probably checked on the weather conditions. Our car's radio gives the weather broadcast, and it predicts a 75% chance of rain, not good!

Wardrobe, lighting, craft services, and all others adapt when an outside shoot becomes an inside one. "Adapt" is their middle name. There are some funny middle names on this set!

Not recognizing the normal path tells me we are heading elsewhere. I forgot, today we do not work at Dream Studios. Ivy shares.

Ivy, "Hey, this morning we're shooting outside. Rain may kick in, so that's why we're shooting the beach scenes first."

Hadley says she and Archer want to swim and collect seashells. Even in his seatbelt Archer jiggles with excitement.

Kristin, an assistant to the director (AD), and actor, has been teaching Hadley about shells. She gave her a shell book, and Hadley, having read the word that means collecting and studying shells, feels professional. Ivy pronounces the word, "conchologist." Hadley is not sure about that funny word, but is happy to know it. Her pronunciation is not quite right, but she still shares her feelings.

Hadley yells, "I'm a conchologist! I'm a conchologist!"

"Yes, you are." Ivy says grinning, "I can't promise, but here's hoping we can swim and go shelling. Shooting the film comes first, but I did pack swimsuits, towels, and sunscreen."

There are many beaches in Southwest Florida. One of the closest from Dream Studios is Fort Myers Beach. Here is hoping we can work and play there today. My home is not far away. It would be cool if my parents could visit.

Ivy says, "Allie, not that you asked, but Mom said she's contacted your parents. They will meet us at the beach. Is that a good thing?"

Allie cheerfully replies, "Ivy, you read my mind! NO, it is not a good thing. It is a GREAT thing! Oh boy!"

Ivy adds, "Mom said the area of the beach where we'll be at allows pets. I'm not sure this was to be a surprise, but guess who your parents will be bringing?"

I screech thinking of Splat my pet goat!

This is a wonderful day!

My family will meet up with us soon. This is excitement with a capital E!

"Allie," Hadley asks, "how did Splat get his name?"

Allie responds, "His furry hair reminded me of black and white splattered paint."

Hadley, "I wondered."

Ivy pulls up to a fast-food drive thru. She does not ask us what we want. I can tell she is on a mission. Bags of food pass through Ivy's window, with most ending up on the floor near my feet. She hands me another bag. In that bag are egg biscuits, two milks, and one juice. Hadley helps Archer before she eats. Ivy continues driving. She will eat on set with the crew.

Ivy explains, "Obviously everyone else won't eat yet, but you can eat now. There will be extra food. Allie, there's enough for your family too."

Allie, with egg biscuit in mouth, muffles, "Thanks Ivy!"

Having full tummies of cereal, Hadley and Archer still find room for milk and egg biscuits. Ivy tells me they will probably eat even more later. After all, they are growing kids!

Looks like the Gulf is ahead. My teacher says that the Gulf of Mexico is a bay. Some call it an ocean. I do. Ivy cracks open windows. We grin, smell fresh salt air and feel the ocean breezes.

Three kids at once, "Yay! We're here!"

Ivy parks. Ahead we see crew setting up. Are we excited, or what?!

Patting my bag insures me that my script notebook is inside. If not, too late!

There is no use looking for my family yet. Ivy reminds me that they probably will not arrive until later. That is okay.

Hadley unbuckles seatbelt, but Archer waits. Ivy reminds Hadley to stay put, as she is about to give safety rules. Archer continues to wait. That little man is so smart.

"Guys," Ivy explains to the little ones, "to begin with, both of you stay close. No one goes near the ocean. That includes you Allie. First, our priority is shooting the film. Allie, you will be told what to do by Deb. Is all understood?"

The two kids yell "Yes!" With my face attached to a juice box, nodding is all one can do while getting the last drop of OJ!

This is not a normal day. Nope, it is movie madness, and we love it!

Chapter 7
Shells & Bells

We scramble out onto the beach enjoying the view with sand under our feet! We pick up sandy shells along the way, and Kristin greets us at the kid-friendly tent. She smiles seeing us and has nice-looking shells for everyone. If we want, later she will paint our names on them!

Christian and Matt are setting up additional tents. Nearby Michayla readies craft services. Under the kid tent there is a blanket spread out. Porta potties are nearby, a bag of toys plus a cooler full of drinks, and snacks are closer. Ivy and Kristin take turns hovering. Today their title is "kid wrangler."

The rest of us stay near our stations. I leave the tent and tag behind Deb. She and Miss Becky consult on wardrobe.

Allie's Movie Adventure

On beaches, anything film-related is a challenge. Sand and salt are archenemies of electronics. Tents with canvas-like walls for the delicate camera equipment were set up first.

Ivy yells, "Allie, come over here please!"

Allie yells back, "I'm on my way!"

Running in sand is not easy. I head to the kid tent as fast as possible. Hadley and Archer are there. She talks to the three of us.

In concerned voice Ivy says, "Hey you guys. Sorry, but I have more instructions."

Archer looks worried.

"Archer," Ivy continues, "don't worry. It is okay; you will have fun today! Making sure you are safe comes first. Okay?"

Archer smiles.

"Okay." Ivy says, "Today an adult, someone you know, will be with you at all times. NO going near water alone or talking to strangers. Got it?"

All three in raised voices, "Yes!"

Suddenly Ivy whips her head toward me. No words, her face speaks volumes. I am just not sure which language!

Allie looking intrigued asks, "Ivy, I said yes to being safe. Is there something else?"

"Yes Allie, there is." Ivy smiles and says, "Look behind you."

Behind me, coming over a sand mound is a small group of people. Even from a distance they look familiar!

The first one popping over the mound is short, black and white, four-legged, and running lickety-split!

A bell rings, and before we know it Splat has jumped mid-air pushing me down, and we roll in the sand. My friends appear happily surprised opening their arms for Splat to jump on them.

A blue leash flaps in the breeze behind Splat's collar. The collar has a little bell with a big sound. Ivy has her eyes and ears on it. She quickly removes the noise maker and hands it to me. Putting it in my pant pocket we continue playing.

Up next should be Mom and Dad. Instead, it is another figure, smallish in size moving at a slow pace. The figure is bent over, reaching for feet that appear to be lost in the sand. It must be Gram!

It is Gram, and behind her is a tall blonde lady who has a rucksack perched atop her back. Only one person I know has that kind of backpack that was a gift from us. Yep, it is Klara!

Czech Republic is Klara's home country, and it is 4,992.5 miles from Southwest Florida. Klara told me that during her first visit. Klara lived with us for months while interning at Dad's veterinary practice. She is majorly cool!

This is an extra big surprise, as we did not know Klara would visit again. She became a vet this year, so now we can call her Doctor Klara. Maybe she will work at Dad's office!

Mom and Dad finally surface. They are carrying beach umbrellas, cooler, towels, and other supplies.

Gram plops down pulling off her shoes, and Klara helps her. Running to them ends up in hugs. Klara takes off her backpack saying there are shells inside it for me and my friends.

Mom must have told Klara that Kristin and Hadley are shellers. So is Klara. There is a bucket of shells at the kid tent. Guessing Kristin did that. It will be great when all the shellers can finally meet.

"Allie," Klara says, "On my first visit here I took home Florida shells, but now I bring you shells from islands all over the world. One is from French Polynesia in the Pacific Ocean. Seeing that you are busy I will give them to your Mom; can't wait until we have time to chat! Okey dokey? Allie, someone is waving, and I bet they need you. I'll see you later."

Allie yells "Ta for now!"

Hearing "okey dokey" is a happy memory. We used to say that all the time when Klara was here last year, and it stuck. Klara was right, they must be about to shoot.

Dad comes to Klara and Gram's rescue. On my way to Deb, I grab my messenger bag at the kid tent. Cool, now Gram, Klara, and my parents can watch me work on a movie set!

Running toward the set I turn and look back. Gram is on her feet. Gram, Klara, Mom, and Dad are waving; I wave back. Splat is with everyone at the kid tent. Next, focus on my work.

About halfway into the shoot Rob the soundman shouts out something to the director.

"Cut!" Eddel yells, "What's wrong?"

"There is a strange noise," says Rob, "and it is ruining the shot. If we were not on a beach, I would say it sounds like a doorbell."

Eddel and Erik loudly say and ask in unison, "That can't be. What is it?!"

Concerned Eddel, "We don't have much good light left, so someone figure out what the sound is and where it's coming from!"

Everyone looks puzzled. Rob's headset stays on hoping he can identify the sound.

Thinking it might be noisy kids I tell Deb. She says it is not that kind of sound. Filming is on pause, and I am hot. Water is needed, but before standing up to get it Deb gives me an odd look. She is about to speak, but Rob beats her to it.

Rob yells, "That's it! It's coming from the area where Allie is. It sounds like a muffled bell. Allie?!"

Oh no! Feeling mortified. Allie yells, "Yes, it's me! My goat's bell is in my pocket. Forgot, sorry."

The bell is removed and thrown toward Ivy. She catches it, carrying it off to Never Neverland. Note to self: "A goat's bell in a pant pocket can be heard by a film's soundman." Seeing a cry coming on, Deb hugs me.

Eddel calls, "Back to one!"

With script notebooks ready we go back to work. No time to cry. The scene wraps. Erik comes up to me.

Erik kindly asks, "The chance of a goat's bell in a pocket on a movie set causing a disturbance is rare, right? By the way, where is that bell?"

Archer asks, "Is this it?"

Allie responds, "No it isn't, but it's a nice shell. Archer, you're a conchologist!"

Archer asks, "I'm a what?"

Archer on the seashore

Chapter 8

Uncle Fizz

A man's voice, "I bet Allie knows where that bell is!"

Heads crank toward the voice.

With a storm soon approaching, the beach has cleared. A few seagulls fly by. One lone man stands barefoot before me. Only I recognize him.

"Uncle Fizz!" Allie yells.

Hugging, he says, "Yep, that's me! I told you whenever you were near water that I would be there, and here I am. It has been too long. How are you? You're taller!"

Uncle Fizz has been my Dad's close friend forever. He knows Dad's brother Uncle Greg and wife Aunt Jackie too. Upon our first meeting we took an immediate shine to each other, and he instantly became my uncle. Uncle Fizz is a scuba diver working underwater discovering shipwrecks and treasure fleets.

Uncle Fizz has told me that fleets came from sea routes' convoy systems. Routes were organized in 1566-1790 by the Spanish Empire. They caused Spain to link with its territories in the Americas across the Atlantic. I memorized it, as one never knows when that kind of information is needed!

My uncle has hunted for treasure almost his whole life. One can find him online, plus he is on television, in videos, and magazines sharing his treasure hunting experiences. He is in books and writes his own. To top it off, he still hunts!

My uncle's nickname comes from his last name, Fismer. The definition of fizz is important to remember. It causes illness in scuba divers. "Fizz" means decompression sickness, and it is when nitrogen forms bubbles in the body. It can cause death. NOT that Carl Fismer wants to have that sickness!

"Uncle Fizz," Allie asks, "Why are you here? By the way, the location of the bell is not known by me. I bet Ivy knows."

Uncle Fizz explains, "Oh, on the bell, and I am here to see you! Erik brought me on as a movie star, so I accepted the film role. Christian shot B-Roll of me down there on the shore. I am kidding about the movie star part. My role is as a scuba diver, and my character swims to shore from an imaginary ship in the Gulf. My scuba gear is over there. Playing that part comes to me naturally, and I wonder why?!"

It's hard to believe Uncle Fizz is here. Erik meanders over saying he knew ahead about the scene. He kept it a secret.

Erik laughing, "Allie, I told Deb to hide it from you in the script. You can be upset at her!"

"Excuse me," Fizz asks Erik, "didn't I interrupt you earlier talking about a bell?"

Erik responds, "No problem, and thanks for working with us. They just told me all the shots are perfect!

If you don't mind though, I need to speak with this young lady for a minute."

Uncle Fizz hugs me and steps back.

What's Erik going to say? Am I kicked off the set...?

"Allie," Erik says calmly, "I meant what I said about the bell. It is something we will not easily forget. Have fun with your family, and feel free to tell your uncle about the bell!"

Whew, kind words from Erik, no surprise.

"Hey, Allie!" Erik turns back around and says, "I hear you're in need of a headshot. In this biz, everyone needs one. Your parents agree, and braces on your teeth make it real!"

Before I know it, I hear click, click, click. Erik directs me. I keep posing until he is happy with the results.

Uncle Fizz runs up posing, making funny faces with me. Done. Now we visit my family, and Uncle Fizz can meet Klara.

Walking off, Erik yells back, "Allie, I'll get the photos to you soon. You can look at them over the weekend, okay?!"

Mom yells, "Thanks Erik! Her photo will officially become a headshot as soon as I add her name and resumé!"

Erik, looking up at the dark sky, waves in agreement to Mom. Seeing the sky, I bet he is thinking it is good that we have already wrapped. He runs to find Archer.

Hadley and Archer become happier conchologists today. Ivy took Hadley swimming, and Kristin and Archer took a walk. They followed a winding beach path that ended at a shoreline away from movie cameras where they played in the ocean and collected shells. Kristin took photos of the beach and shells. Erik visited to take a shot of Archer riding his "dolphin."

Playing & shelling on the beach!

Allie's Movie Memories

My movie friends at their creative best!

Deb, top left & right as film characters
Miss Becky as model & wardrobe supervisor
Prana Songbird on stage & in film

Deb as crew on a SW Florida beach film set
Stunt dogs - Jazzy, Baxter & Dolly

Splat & Erik... Here we goat again!

The Mizner Estate (1924)
Film screenshot of car entering the estate
Erik on drone – Estate's former Grande Ballroom

Musicians

Photo: Louis Blackwell 2018/2019
Bridget Kelly & Tim Fik
of The Bridget Kelly Band

Shaw Davis & The Black Ties
(permission to use both images by
Marlene Palumbo)

More Musicians

© Rob Whitehurst (Permission to use by Rob Whitehurst)
Rob on stage as bass player or bassist.
He is our movie's soundman, nicknamed
"Soundman to the stars!"

Peter Noone of Herman's Hermits
(Permission to use by Peter Noone)
Mom is his #1 fan!
CJ Morgan as "Dolly" (for Dad)

Allie's Movie Adventure

Deb is a member of the Peter Noone Fan Club!

Purple Christmas card from Peter Noone
Inside is red handwriting

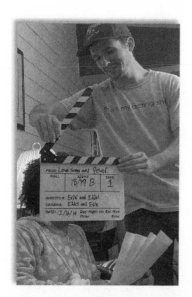

Slates or Clapboards
Christian and Prana - Deb in mask
Deb using slate with a Superhero!

Captain Uncle Fizz hard at work!

(Permission given to use this & all his images of/by Carl Fismer)

Comedy aside, Captain Fizz is a real boat captain
licensed at Master Level, the highest level that can
be obtained allowing him to perform captain duties
as well as operate inspected vessels (100 tons),
AND he's an author!

On & Off Movie Sets

At makeup station - Prana & Ivy, Hadley & Ivy
Me on scooter during film shoot break
Archer the artist

"Open Up"
Poem & Art by Calder (age 7)

Calder is Miss Becky's family member.
Here Calder tells how she feels about wanting to get
out of her house during COVID-19.

An "old ship," a cruise ship, & Uncle Fizz

Results of Conchologist/Sheller

Photos: Kristin Mercedes Bence

collected & photographed
by Kristin

Checking out future film locations

Deb & Miss Becky at wardrobe station,
at back left are changing tents/portable wardrobes

Erik & Eddel on banner
Prana at mic with fellow actor Kevin Mayle
Prana models new fashion design by
Vic of Victor Miller Designs - Photo of me by Erik

Behind the Scenes with
Kristin, Deb, Rose, Matt, Sparkles, Prana...
don't ya just love selfies?!

Miss Becky on photo shoot
Photo by: K'Tography
aka Kati Heysinger Photography

Working on sets are sound/boom, slate,
producer, cameraman, director, actors...

Me in kitchen
Cast & Crew
My pals & I read

COOL movie screenshot of Prana as Violet
Sparkles with actors Ivan & Prana in screenshot

Monitors

Me

Prana

Vocal Rehearsal

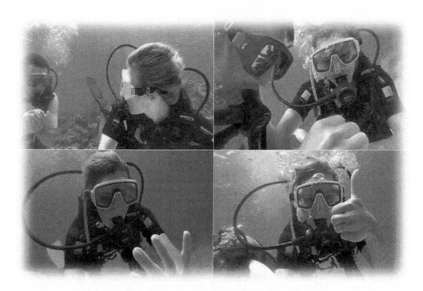

Boris & Klara discover shells, "a rock,"
... and turtles underwater!

Relaxing After Filming

My pals and I enjoy the beach after the film wraps.

Archer on beach learns he is a conchologist/sheller
Archer must be thinking, "I'm a what?"
Dr. Klara on holiday
Uncle Fizz with wristband I gave him

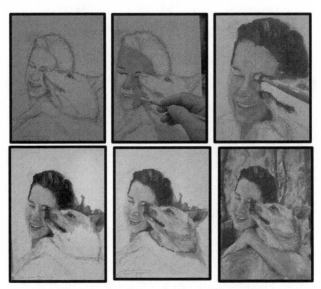

Progressive Anna Art
(painted in color)
by Roger Kabler

Family photo of Rusty Brown

Chapter 9
Kodiak, Anna & Rusty

As we head back to Dream Studios I think of the day's events. Beach scenes wrapped successfully. Captain "Uncle" Fizz sailed off. Before leaving on his imaginary boat, he learned the true story of Splat's bell. That story caused him to laugh and apologize all at the same time. Uncle Fizz promised next time we would take a REAL boat ride. After we hug, my barefooted uncle with shoes in hand, takes off down the beach.

Weather threatens my family's picnic. After taking a few bites, we pack up, run, and reach the car in the nick of time. Klara has already taken Gram to the car, and they picnic in the back seat. After throwing beach supplies into the trunk, we jump in hearing rain drizzling on the car's hood, followed by a gushing downpour.

Mom behind the steering wheel, "No worries, this looks like one of those rains that will be over in a few of minutes."

Sure enough, the rain soon stops, or we have driven out of it. Either way, Dad's office emergency service calls.

One of Dad's clients will meet him at his vet clinic. In veterinary medicine the client is the owner of the pet, and the pet is the patient. Since it is after hours, Dad's staff will not be there. Klara volunteers, and I will be helpful too.

We get home and unload some of the car's contents like the picnic basket, Splat, Mom, and Gram. As Dad backs out of the driveway Mom yells that she will contact Dunky saying that we may be late for the tour.

Hopefully, this will not be an all-nighter!

On the way, Dad discovers the patient is a young male husky itching and broken out in hives. Dad guesses it is a bite from a venomous, or poisonous, insect. Klara thinks wasps or hornets are the guilty party. If that is the case, we hope he was not attacked by an aggressive swarm.

As we pull into the office, we see the family waiting. Kodiak is four months old. The pup has been a patient of Dad's since birth. We see him scratching and whining, poor Kodiak.

After the pup and his large family enter the office, we three do our thing. Kodiak and family wait in the lobby. Dr. Klara makes sure the largest exam room is ready. Dad turns on lights while speaking to the family.

My job is getting Kodiak's medical record. The family seems nervous, and Dr. Klara puts them at ease. With his record in hand, she asks everyone to follow her.

Dr. Klara examines the pup. The prognosis proves to be correct, with the diagnosis being one venomous insect bite.

A syringe of diphenhydramine is prepared by Dad. He explains that it is an antihistamine for relieving symptoms of allergies, including insect bites. It is for motion sickness too, which is good for any pet not used to traveling.

Dr. Klara gives Kodiak the shot. Both doctors observe him looking for signs of shock. After several minutes, the doctors agree that Kodiak is good to go. Everyone is relieved. Dad suggests ways of helping rid their yard and home of poisonous insects. He tells them we do the same thing at our home.

If the family is okay with it, Dad says I can get a photo with Kodiak. They agree, and Dr. Klara takes it.

The family has three kids, two boys and a girl. The daughter's name is Cora, and she looks my age. When Cora is not busy with Kodiak, her family, and school, she says she likes to cook.

Kodiak and me
at Dad's office

When the family first arrived, Cora was upset, they all were. Everyone is better now, especially Kodiak!

With the exam room spotless, paperwork done, lights off, and office locked up, we head home. Dad calls Mom. She, Gram, and Splat are ready.

It is early evening by the time we roll onto Dream Studios' gravel driveway. No doubt Dunky and his pups will welcome us. They live next door, and Erik called asking for the front door to be unlocked. Splat will play outside.

My folks already had a tour, but Gram and Klara have not. If Dunky is okay with it, the next tour is by me!

Like sand, gravel is a challenge to walk on. Klara helps Gram, and all of us enter through the front door.

After Dad parks, he takes Splat out back to join the chickens. Mom comes with us. We wait for Dad near the soundboard. Dunky and Rita come inside where they meet Gram and Klara.

Dunky says, "I usually give the tours, but I think Allie knows this place like the back of her hand. Enjoy!"

Mom, "Thanks Dunky. Will let you know when we're done."

Before Dunky and Rita leave, their dogs Rusty and Anna come up to sniff us. Klara says they smell Kodiak. The dogs go up to Gram, but we made sure she was seated first.

Rita says fair-haired Anna can be a little overprotective. Rusty, being part Hound, is bigger but has a calmer nature. He was named due to his hair color.

Little do Dunky's farm animals and dogs know that two veterinarians, Dr. Anderson and Dr. Klara, are here tonight.

Dunky has said that Rusty and Anna have always been healthy. He thinks it is from playing with Sparkles and chasing the chickens. Dunky lets the dogs outside, and they join Splat running in the backyard.

Through windows, we watch the critters play. The couple goes outside and joins their pups, then the four of them return home for the night.

A Dream Studios' tour by Allie is about to begin!

Chapter 10

Soundman to the Stars

The closest entrance to Dream Studios' sound, vocal, and drum rooms are located at the building's front side where we entered. It is good seeing Gram taking things in. Visiting here must be a treat for her, as she grew up in a musical home.

Dad and Klara have not come in yet. They are still checking on Splat. Mom is about to go outside herself when she sees the doorknob turn.

Klara and Dad enter. We are five minutes into my "tour talk" when Mom and Gram ask where the lady's room is. I tell them it is on the other side of the building. Dad agrees to come along. Klara follows looking at everything along the way.

As we hike toward the bathroom, the tour continues. Seeing various recording rooms makes for interesting chatter.

At the bathroom they notice it is a one-seater. Gram goes first. While waiting, my plan is to look for Splat outside through a window. Opening a window curtain reveals his face is flush up to the windowpane. He must have heard our voices. He looks funny!

Dad yells, "Close the curtain!"

We can tell Dad is worried about Splat. It has gotten dark, so Dad and Klara go back outside to visit our little goat from Africa.

After bathroom visits are over, we wait for our vets. Mom calls out the back door, but there is no response.

Dad and Klara return through another door.

"Remember Allie," Dad says, "Splat is a pet. He does not know he was born to be a farm animal. The chickens roosted, and Sparkles went to the barn. Splat was alone, so we put him in the car."

Allie says, "We know Dad, figured that's what you were up to."

Klara was most likely polite and went along with Dad. She winks at us indicating she did.

While Dad uses the restroom, Gram checks out the green room's kitchen. She has a question.

Gram asks, "Why is this kitchen small?"

She does not understand what a green room is. Klara says that their kitchen at home is about this size, but it is big enough for their family.

"Gram," Allie explains, "this building isn't a home, rather it's designed for entertainers to work in. This is all they need in a kitchen."

Gram, "I see."

Allie continues, "The small refrigerator is run off either electricity or batteries. It holds a few drinks and snacks. Paper supplies are in the cupboards above."

Gram, "Oh, understood. Thanks Allie, and I am proud of you working on a film set. This is your first adventure without family. I have heard that you use the word 'framily.' It's the combination of friend and family, right?"

Gram gives hugs. All of us agree about framily and my working away from home. Klara, of course, travels alone thousands of miles visiting people she has never met. Yes, she is over twice my age. That helps.

My parents say it is time to leave. First, the bathroom gets two more visitors. We will continue the tour, finishing from where we started.

Before leaving, we visit the big room used for setting up. Mom and Dad have seen it, but it is new to Gram and Klara. Pointing to the wardrobe station, makeup and hair, piano, and the stage are a lot to take in. Gram notices posters on the walls.

Mom flips out, "I didn't notice that poster before! That is Peter Noone! He's from Herman's Hermits, and he was or IS Herman!"

Allie adds, "Oh! Deb is a huge fan of Peter Noone too, and she is a member of his fan club. What a coincidence."

PETER NOONE OF HERMAN'S HERMITS FAME

Dad remarks, "Calm down Honey. Although is there a 'Dolly' poster up there?"

We laugh at my parents who are blushing. Gram wants to continue the tour. She surprises me asking about acoustics.

Allie says, "This building was designed to produce high quality music and vocals. Good acoustics are necessary for professional results. Prana tells me that acoustics consist of the properties or qualities of a room or building. There's more, but that's the gist."

Gram smiles. She plays the piano, so she knows about acoustics.

Klara asks, "May I take photos?"

Allie, "That is a good idea. Let's take selfies too!"

While we hike to the front everyone takes several photos throughout Dream Studios.

People suddenly file in. It looks like it is a band, and they are here for rehearsals. Dunky enters behind them apologizing.

Dunky says, "Sorry. I forgot the schedule. You don't have to, but are you leaving soon?"

Dad says we are. Gram interrupts and asks if she can stay and listen to the band.

Dad and Dunky say, "Sure you can."

Dunky leaves the room, and we take seats across from the soundboard. It is the perfect view through a large glass panel between us and the band. We watch them set up.

Klara takes more photos, and Gram looks bewildered. All this is new to her, but it was her idea to stay. We hope Gram does not change her mind. We know Gram; she will like it!

Gram is from old school. She stares at the tattoos and ponytails. Except for men getting tattoos in the military, she is not used to seeing them. She is especially not used to seeing men in ponytails. We catch her cracking a smile.

Gram turns up her hearing aids. Oh no, that may not be wise. The band should not be too loud with the thick glass between us. We will see what happens.

Dad says, after we leave here, getting food on our way home is on the agenda. We all agree. Mom leaves to get the car, and Klara goes with her. If Splat is awake, he needs to be walked; Klara will walk him.

My only assignment is to get Gram to the car. Dad wants to find and thank Dunky. Those are two good ideas, but mine has failed. I cannot find Gram!

We are here longer than planned. The band is breaking down, and Dunky will need to lock up. Dad finds him, thanks him, and goes to the car.

My search for Gram is still unsuccessful. Maybe Gram is in the back. Nope, no Gram. Turning on an outside light there is no sign of Gram out there either.

The loading dock shows no sign of Gram. My peeking into the big set up room reveals... no Gram.

Getting desperate, I head back up front to tell my folks who are still waiting in the car. On the way, a band member stops me asking if I have seen Rob. The band member tells me that he is the soundman for our film.

Allie says, "No, I have not seen Rob but will look for him. Have you seen my Gram?"

Band member, "Rob is our bassist, and if you see him tell him we're leaving. I will keep an eye out for your Gram."

At this point, desperate, I am considering getting help. Gram is lost!

Upon entering the sound room on my way out, there she is! Gram and Rob are on the couch busy chatting.

The colors they are wearing blend into the furniture which caused me to miss them when passing by earlier. They are so busy chatting they do not even notice me.

"Gram!" Allie speaks loudly, "Sorry to interrupt, but everyone is in the car ready to leave. Hi Rob. Oh Rob, a band member was looking for you. They are leaving too."

Rob jumps up to run, but he turns back to help Gram to her feet. Each gives hugs goodbye.

The musician grabs his guitar and leaves. We do too. Gram gets in the front seat, and it is easy to see she feels bad that everyone was waiting for her.

Gram says apologetically, "Sorry, someone told me to wait on the couch, and one of you would get me. She told me that I shouldn't walk on the gravel alone."

Dad asks who said that.

"I don't know," says Gram, "but I'm glad I waited, as Rob and I chatted. Were you aware that he is a soundman and bass guitarist?"

In the car my seat is behind Dad and next to Klara. Gram may be talking, but all I think of is food. Mom is on the opposite side winding down her window.

Dad stops, as someone is running up. It is Dunky and Rita with Rusty and Anna. Gram and Rita wave to each other.

Rita says to Mom, "Glad you found her."

Whispering, Rita says, "Sorry, I just texted you about your mother. In it, I say she seemed tired, so I had her stay on the couch until you got her. When she and Rob began chatting, I left knowing she was in good hands."

Mom, "Thank you Rita. Sounds like my mother had a great time. Thanks again!"

Gram, "I did!"

Dunky starts to talk about his dogs. Even though we are hungry, we do not interrupt him. He says Rusty, in his day, could run as fast as a greyhound. Anna still looks, runs, and jumps like a deer.

Dunky says, "Allie, so you'll be shooting in the studios again soon, good! See you then."

Allie, "Oh. Thanks again, and goodnight!"

We wave, and Dad heads out. Through all of it, Splat remains asleep. Klara walked and fed him, so he is set for the night. Gram keeps our minds off food and tells us more about Rob.

Gram says, "Law enforcement is in Rob's family, and he almost became a sheriff. Instead, he became an entertainer in front of and behind the scenes. Rob plays in bands as a bassist. As you know Allie, he is your film's soundman. If you cannot tell, I am excited to have met him. He has a family too."

With enthusiasm Gram says, "I asked him, and Rob said he doesn't have tattoos. We both agree that he is probably the only musician in the world who does not have one."

Gram continues to share about Rob. She tells us that by working with celebrities he earned the nickname…
"Soundman to the Stars."

Mom says it has been an interesting day. Gram agrees, and she asks if it is okay that she cooks something for us at home tonight.

Gram, "I felt tired earlier this evening, but since chatting with Rob I am more awake!"

Mom offers to help with the cooking. We all like that idea too, especially Gram. Dad will be taking me to Ivy so no eating with the family. I do not say anything; it won't do any good.

"Allie," Dad says, "Erik texted your mom earlier. He told her that he has a lot of editing to do, so everyone has a few days off. Your grandma is staying with us over the weekend. Klara is staying with the Brown family down the road from us, but she will visit us some too. Is all that okay with you?"

Silence... Gram reaches over the back of the seat and touches my knee. She tells me to say yes. I do.

Gram used to draw. On the way home she talks about sketching Rob from a photo he gave her. If she sketches him, I will have her sign it and send it to him, "Soundman to the Stars!"

Chapter 11

Many Colors

We drop Klara off. She promises to visit us this weekend.

It has been several weeks since my last visit home. Approaching the driveway, I take it all in. We unload at the front door. Splat is sound asleep. Dad says he will bring him in after he puts the car in the garage.

Inside, Mom and Gram prepare soup and sandwiches. Dad carries Splat inside and puts him in his kennel, but Splat wakes up. I climb in with him.

In the kennel Splat places his head on my lap, and I pet his soft fur. It brings back memories from Kenya, Africa.

Splat soon begins to snore. After all, he has had a long day; all of us have.

Getting into my own bed sounds good, but food first. Tonight, we enjoy a tasty treat. Where Klara is staying, she is free to use the neighbor's kitchen, so maybe she will get herself a bite to eat too. We look forward to seeing more of her.

Mom asks, "Allie, would you like friends over tomorrow? Your Dad could grill chicken. Gram and I enjoy making your favorites, like potato salad, homemade rolls, a veggie tray, and chocolate mousse with whip cream and strawberries on top!"

Allie happily shouts, "It all sounds great! Thanks!"

Tonight's soup and sandwich hit the spot. Teeth and bed are next, will shower in the morning. Before going to sleep I sit on my bed enjoying the view. My room looks the same as I left it. Goodnight room.

Awaking to bright lights I head to the bathroom. While in the shower, Gram makes my bed. I can tell it is her from the lingering scent of perfume, my favorite. After quickly getting dressed I run downstairs to find Splat and enjoy breakfast.

Blueberries are yet another scent in the air. Blueberry pancakes, yay! Oh no, the hall clock says it is 11:30. No surprise that bright lights filled my room. It is almost midday sunshine. I do not want to waste another sunray!

In the kitchen Gram says, "Allie, morning. Since you have been rising early lately, we let you sleep. Come join us!"

We chow down pancakes. Mom remembered fresh fruit, juice, and an abundance of baby marshmallows that melt into a solid white layer atop my hot cocoa!

Plans for the afternoon are shared, but my plan right now is to play with Splat. Rushing out of the kitchen no one gets a chance to tell me about our pet. However, Splat's snoring tips me off that he is asleep.

"Dad!" Allie yells, "Is Splat okay?! He's still asleep!"

"Allie," Dad says, "I bet you think Splat slept in. He slept through the night, played hard earlier this morning, and now he is napping. I'm sure he'll be ready to play again soon."

Allie calmer, "Okey dokey, that sounds good. Dad, I hung up my raincoat in the hall closet and saw an outfit in there with four leg holes. What?"

Dad explains, "Yes, and it's very colorful too! Here is the scoop. Your grandma wanted Splat to have his own clothes, at least a hand sewn outfit, so she made him one.

"After she left, we put it on him. Since he did not look comfortable, we put it away. We have not told Gram, so please do not tell her. We will eventually."

"Don't worry," Allie adds, "she won't hear it from me. Although it can be said, Splat is a goat of many colors!"

Dad and I laugh waking Splat up. Both his eyes pop open at once, then he stands waiting to get out. He runs circles around me. We play in the yard until I feel tired. What?! Me tired? Must be all the hard film work.

"Allie!" Mom shouts, "Our guests will be here soon. It is okay to take a nap. One of us will wake you when they arrive."

Gram sees me watching her hold up a finger to her lips. She points to the hall closet. We meet there.

"Shhh," Gram whispers, "since Splat is your goat, I thought you should know this. Your folks do not know that I know. Gram reaches deeply into the closet telling me she made this to keep Splat warm. She pulls out his little coat. It is the same one Dad showed me, but I don't tell her.

Smiling, Gram says, "I'm happy to adjust this if it doesn't fit, okay? It is a coat. Better yet, it is a goat of many colors. Not sure everyone will catch the biblical reference, but we do!"

Allie hugs Gram, "I love it, and I love you."

After dropping off for a nap, hoof steps awaken me. Knowing that Splat likes to sleep on the floor near my bed, he must have dragged a towel upstairs and dropped it there.

Rolling to the bed's edge to get a better look, I see no towel. Instead, it is a goat of many colors!

Allie says, "Here we goat again!"

Chapter 12

Chleba

I wake up to voices. Could it be Ivy or the kids telling me to get up? No, it can't be. I panic for a moment wondering where my on-set bag is.

It is not Ivy's voice. It belongs to Gram!

Another voice in the room is one not heard for a while. It belongs to Mrs. Batzing, my school principal!

Mrs. Batzing says, "Everyone downstairs can just wait. I decided to come up and see you Allie. I'm looking forward to hearing what you've been up to on the movie set!"

Mrs. Batzing gives hugs before returning downstairs. Dad is seen shortly after at my door.

Dad says, "Allie, before you say anything to your friends about working on the movie, we need to talk."

Nodding to Dad, my reflection catches in the mirror. This outfit will not do!

After my shower I see that my bed is made again, and a change of clothes is neatly laid on it. That's Gram for you!

All dressed I head downstairs to find Dad. In the dining room and kitchen there's food set out everywhere. Mom and Gram have prepared a feast!

Dad comes running.

Dad, rather excited, says, "Allie, after I heard what Mrs. Batzing said I thought we had better talk, but now I'm cooking chicken. How about chatting later, okay?"

Allie responds, "Agreed, Dad."

Speaking of food, Klara walks in with arms full. Whatever she is carrying smells good. She signals me to meet in the kitchen. There is not much space on the counter, so she plops her backpack down in a corner.

"Allie," Klara says, "Yesterday I was busy baking. I made chleba (kleba, with soft vowels). In Czech Republic we call bread chleba. I even looked up its history for you; I knew you would ask. This is made from one of my mother's favorite recipes."

Allie says, "Klara, thank you! It looks and smells delicious. Everyone will love it, and here are baskets to hold a couple loaves."

"I'm not through yet." says Klara smiling.

From her backpack Klara pulls out a cloth bag. Inside it are two bunches of brown paper. Klara places the paper on the counter's edge. She smiles as if thinking of something.

"Wrapping things up nicely," Klara says, "runs in our family. I carried these gifts all the way from my mother in Czech Republic."

The paper bunches reveal two gift-wrapped packages. We each unwrap one. She unwraps homemade butter, and I unwrap seedless raspberry preserves in a fancy jar. Wow!

Klara slices and puts aside two pieces of warm bread. She cuts the rest for guests, putting chleba in baskets under linen towels. The extra loaves are placed in the pantry. Without asking permission, we eat slices of buttered chleba!

"The bread and preserves," says Klara, "are my family's favorites. My mother taught me how to make them. I'm happy to teach you, all of you."

Klara tells me that while I was gone, she made mashed potatoes and cookies for my family, and we can make them later together. She gave my mother and Gram the recipes.

Mom and grandma enter the kitchen looking happily surprised. They knew Klara would be bringing food, but they were not sure what.

Gram asks, "Allie, did you get the recipe for the bread, I mean chleba?"

Allie, "Not yet, but soon we'll have the bread's history. Recipes come later, and I'd like Klara's other recipes she gave you and Mom, thanks!"

"Klara," Allie says, "here's an idea. Online we can share recipes. Our blog's name could be something like 'Klara & Allie's International Cooking Network.'"

Klara, "Good, but how about your name first?"

Klara hands me a folded paper containing the history of chleba. Mom borrows it.

Allie says, "Thanks Klara!"

Klara responds, "My boyfriend Boris helped me translate it into English. I hope you can read it. I will give you the recipe. Recipes aren't as easy to translate, but I'll figure it out."

Mom unfolds the paper of chleba history that came all the way from Czech Republic. She will make copies of it later. It reads:

History of Chleba

Chleba or bread was historically fundamental to a traditional carb-heavy, winter-proof Czech diet. Chleba is not of Czech origin. It comes from the Germanic word "hlaiba" - chleb or chleba is common among the Slavic languages, as is the vast array of sourdough bread recipes.

Chapter 13
Silent Witness

In the kitchen, my favorite foods are seen on every nook and cranny. Friends, neighbors, and loved ones mingle.

Dad wants to chat with me about my work. Those here know about my summer job. Telling details about the movie has remained a secret. With me not at home, no one has thought to ask about what I do. Now they ask.

Movie details not to be shared are shoot locations, the film's storyline, and the actors' names. Being home makes it more difficult keeping those secrets.

Silent witness is my, rather our, new job description. We can see but cannot say. On her own, Gram marches into the music room with people following her like sheep. Gram does not know Mom is behind her with a tray full of chocolate mousse cups!

Before others ask more questions, Dad and I need to find a place to have a private chat. Dad's office ends up being that place.

Dad says, "Allie, I have a plan. We will go out front and make an announcement. After we share what you do and why you cannot talk about it, I am sure our guests will understand. Remember, none of these people have worked on a film. It is okay for you to be a silent witness."

After we practice what to say we get everyone together. Dad tells Mom what we are up to, and she smiles telling us Gram has a plan too. Klara comes toward us looking a bit puzzled. We fill her in. She has been on film sets, so she knows the scoop. Poor Gram missed the briefing. At a fast clip, for Gram, she comes up to us.

With shortened breath Gram says, "My piano playing was to help gather everyone in one place for you. It worked for a while, but when the mousse was gone, they were too! Does anyone have any more ideas?!"

We begin to laugh but look at each other realizing Gram meant well. Mom fills Gram in on Dad's plan. Gram laughs at herself. Dad has Gram play a couple of loud piano chords to get the guests' attention. From our staircase, Dad speaks.

Dad says, "Thank you for being interested in what Allie is doing this summer. She, all of us, appreciate that. However, Allie is not allowed to talk about certain things. She and the other cast and crew are sworn to secrecy. Everyone had to sign an agreement. Thanks for your patience. Direct any questions you might have to me. Let's have fun!"

Gram plays the piano again, and no mousse is needed. The adults gather around and sing, and the kids play with me and Splat in the backyard.

A couple of my friends ask me questions about the film. I remind them that I cannot share right now but will later.

As darkness approaches, we go out in the front yard to enjoy the ballpark's fireworks. They are breathtaking. A table on our porch offers self-serve popcorn and drinks. What a great ending to the day.

As the fireworks say goodnight, so do the guests. Mrs. Batzing hangs out introducing us to Miss Dotty, my new teacher this fall.

Miss Dotty tells me she has learned from Mrs. Batzing all about using journals in the classroom and how Splat attended her wedding. His nose in the cake is her favorite story.

Allie says, "Yes, it was embarrassing that our goat's nose was covered in icing. It makes for a good story though, and we're still telling it!"

Everyone has left. Klara helps us clean up in the kitchen. Sweeping and taking out the trash are my jobs.

Before heading to bed, I send Splat kisses in the air. He has not learned how to return them yet, but that is okay.

With one day left before returning to set, my plan is to get up earlier in hopes of enjoying a longer day. Heading up the staircase I enjoy looking at the wall covered in photo memories.

Photos on the wall reveal family members dating back before Gram. At the base of the staircase Gram looks up at me with a thoughtful face. Like me, Gram is another silent witness.

Chapter 14

Back on Set

Today is Sunday. After attending church, we have a quiet day here at home. Enjoying Splat and my human family is not to be taken for granted. Klara visits bringing her mom's chleba/bread recipe. We eat sandwiches with slices of chleba.

Monday morning arrives fast. We take our time eating breakfast. After playing with Splat, it is time to return to the movie set. Splat and Klara will remain here. Later, Klara goes to the beach with friends for shelling and swimming.

With Gram returning to her home, Klara will stay with us. Dad is going to put an extra bed in the guest room. That way, two guests can visit at the same time, lately it is Gram and Klara.

Dr. Klara stays with us at least until summer's end, and she will help Dad at the office and get in a lot of beach time too.

Dad knows how to get to Dream Studios by heart. There is no hurrying, and no need to get there by sunrise like everyone else. Heather told Mom that mid-morning is fine. Dad shoots for 9:00 a.m.

Dunky said we would be shooting at Dream Studios again. He was right. We arrive promptly at 8:55 a.m.

As we pull in, familiar faces are seen unloading vehicles. Others must be busy inside setting up. Before jumping out of the car it is hugs and kisses all around, and ta for now. I carry two bags today, and one is my big lunch bag made by Gram.

In the past, when living with Gram during school days, she packed my lunches. My school friends wanted to trade theirs for mine. No way.

Cellophane or tinfoil were newly invented when Gram was young, and it was probably expensive. She has always used, and continues to use, wax paper. It was invented in 1876.

Gram uses wax paper on sandwiches, pickles, and even desserts. That kind of paper, when folded properly, seals each food perfectly. Wrapped items are placed inside a paper bag with zero leakage. If there was a contest for wax paper wrapping, she would win!

Gram did not give me a drink today. She knows drinks are provided on set, and that craft services has a variety to choose from. Plus there are snacks and light meals. Caterers are used sometimes too. They offer hot food choices 1-3 times a day. Today is not one of them.

On all my first days of school Mom posed me, bag in hand, standing next to my red bike. Today is like that, but instead I pose at the car with two bags in hand, a script girl's and the brown paper kind.

Dad begins to drive off but stops the car. He rolls down the window.

Dad's words are in the air, "Allie, Erik will keep us posted where you're shooting. We may return to visit; we will let you know. We love you. Be safe!"

Eyes flood as our car drives out of sight. Hearing sweet Miss Becky's voice cheers me up. Swiftly she walks my way.

Miss Becky screeches, "Welcome back Allie!"

Homesick tears dissolve. Her kind words and a hug were what I needed.

Allie responds happily, "Hi! Glad to be back!"

Miss Becky and I unload her car. With arms full we head inside. Miss Becky sets up her station. I put my two bags down before checking in with Deb. Will tell everyone later that Gram packed chleba and butter for everyone.

Rose arrives. She always has a smile, and she never keeps it to herself. Today Rose wears a dark pantsuit, as her character is a bodyguard. In real life she was a New York City (NYC) police officer. She has retired, but she keeps busy. Rose has always been interested in acting. Now she tries her hand at it and is loving it!

Like Deb, Rose is another perfect example of a serious and professional actor. She trained, got a headshot, agent, and experience.

Deb gets my attention and tells me we are not needed on set for a while. With that in mind, my camera finds its way back out the door. Rose and Deb come along.

Photos cannot be shared with social media yet, but it will be nice having them to enjoy now and use later. No one says photos cannot go in my journal. Before going back in, the three of us shoot several photos and videos. We cannot take photos on set, but Heather, Ivy, and Kristin can. They'll give us copies.

From outside, we see background actors entering the green room. We go inside.

Miss Becky is looking at her notes. She needs to know which actors should be checked first. She asks if they have their wardrobe with them versus in their cars.

In a low voice Miss Becky says, "I know some of these extras, and they seldom bring their clothes inside. They wait until they are told, even though they have been sent emails with instructions telling them what to do."

Allie says, "Exactly. I got that email myself."

Miss Becky adds, "It's not good when actors are needed on set, but their clothes aren't approved yet. Like today, cars are parked far away, and if it rains clothes get wet!"

Allie in agreement, "Yes, having a simple garbage bag on hand to keep clothes dry is a nice idea, but I guess no one thinks of such things!"

"Allie," Miss Becky says, "if my voice sounds upset it's not at you. When feeling this way, I say, Whaaaaat?!"

Miss Becky asks the small group again if their wardrobe is here with them. She sees that most do not have their clothes. There's silence. Miss Becky returns to her station taking one prepared actor with her.

In the doorway I peek around the corner at the extras. Sure enough, people jump up rushing out of the green room tripping over each other. Most likely they are fetching their clothes, or there is a fire we don't know about!

Allie asks, "Miss Becky, what do you think of unprepared actors?"

Miss Becky, "What?!!!!!"

Saying that, has become a joke we share. The extras are lucky to have Miss Becky.

A few more who have clothes with them are called to the wardrobe station. Even though these people have the correct choice of clothes, which was emailed to them, most of the clothes are wrinkled! I say to myself, "What?!"

It is easy to see who the professionals are, and they are checked and excused first. Those with wrinkled clothes give Miss Becky more work. It is more to steam - the clothes, not the people!

"Allie," says Miss Becky, "actors don't realize that some of us crew keep mental and written notes of people who are unprepared or difficult to work with. Trouble is, those who are not called back, seldom know why. Not sure it would even help."

Miss Becky has two steamers. They are intended to be used only on the main actors' clothes. Multiple changes make it difficult for lead actors to maintain everything. Rehearsals and shooting keep them busy.

My offering to help steam is turned down. Miss Becky does not want me burned. Heather and Ivy jump in to help. Heather and Deb brought steamers, so that is four when one should be enough!

When not steaming, Miss Becky sews buttons, mends, and adjusts garments that may be too big or too small. She makes certain actors wear the right outfits in the correct scenes, and she takes photos for that reason. Of course, the wardrobe department is not the only one with challenges.

A film's electrical department uses batteries, chargers, extension cords, and electricity. When the power is down, pre-charged batteries help, but they last only a few hours.

In the twentieth century, celluloid film on reels was used. It is seldom used now-a-days. Some people on this set are old enough to remember, and they probably do not miss it. There are exceptions.

Real film is what this quote refers to, "on the cutting room floor." It means the floor is where unused film goes that is not used in a finished movie, and no one wants to be on the floor!

Film editors or continuity crew who catch and fix errors all day long see movies and television shows in a different way. Maybe they learn to ignore seeing the mistakes, so they can enjoy the movie.

Eddel and Erik give the main or principal actors time to rehearse. There are two actors rehearsing outside now.

When moviegoers view a film, it is easy to assume the actors know each other in real life. In many cases, they have never met. The use of green screen, or special effects, makes it seem as if actors have physically worked together, but they have not.

Actors who have not met on set tend to first meet at Red Carpet events or on TV talk shows. Such actors may say to each other on a show, "It is nice to finally meet you!"

There may be a lot going on, but it is great being back on set!

Chapter 15
Pieces of History

On our way to the next shoot the two of us squeeze into Miss Becky's car. We have the cast's wardrobe, so getting there early to set up is crucial.

My family and history books say that today's location represents a piece of history. We will relive it in person and maybe make our own!

So far, *Love Song and Power* has shot in Florida and Georgia. For this film, there has been no shooting in a mansion until today.

We will shoot at an historical site called The Mizner Estate. It is a small part of Florida's history but an historical adventure just the same.

Allie recollects, "Miss Becky, this estate was built in 1924. It housed many residents. My great grandmother was born the year before this mansion was built, and her family lived close by."

Miss Becky exclaims, "That's amazing! I'm told over the years many families have lived in this mansion, and even a business worked out of it."

As we get close to the estate, a dual gate is coming up ahead. It has a gold lion-like crest on each side. A code is entered, and the gates open. I watch each gate close behind us. Up ahead crew members can be seen unloading and setting up. We park and begin to unload Miss Becky's car.

It is fun envisioning people from another time in history. Photographs can help bring the past back to life. Mom said she will be looking through Great Gram's albums for old photos of this era and from this area.

Trying to imagine their vehicles, clothes, culture, and more is "surreal." That word means almost unbelievable, and that's how I feel right now. When the mansion was new it was part of the 1920's heyday era. The mansion looks like it did a century ago, and that is thanks to those who maintained it.

Miss Becky shares, "Erik says we're allowed to take photo memories."

With arms full, we head to the backside of this beautiful estate. It is called a solarium. Setting up is next, and time is of the essence. Walking with our arms full, Erik runs toward us to help. The three of us must look like pack animals!

Erik leads the way, and we can tell he is anxious to talk. Our ears are perked.

"Doreen Lehner (lay-ner)," Erik says, "is this mansion's current owner and resident. She says historical records show the mansion's namesake to be an American resort architect of Mediterranean Revival and Spanish Colonial Revival style. The architect's name was Addison Cairns Mizner, and he left an impression on South Florida

Erik says, "Mizner died in 1933 at age 66, but his work continues to impress. Some may think that is boring, but I think it is cool.

The Mizner Estate's front grounds & solarium in back

Miss Becky says, "I love hearing all this!"

Erik tells us, "Thanks to Doreen, recently this piece of history has been improved and maintained. Its sturdy exterior keeps an historical look, and its interior design and decor reflects days gone by. Doreen, herself, is a part of history too. Her military title is that of Senior Chief, Hospital Corpsman, US Navy, Retired. Plus, she is a hero!"

"Amazing!" Allie shouts.

"One photo I've seen," adds Erik, "shows Doreen with an Iraqi patient in a helicopter being airlifted from a burning oil platform. There are many photos, articles, and video footage on this famous lady."

Allie says, "Knowing we were coming my dad discovered a lot about Doreen online and in books!"

Erik asks, as we continue to work, "Miss Becky, didn't you say Allie's family has history in this part of town?"

Miss Becky, "Yes Erik, some of Allie's distant relatives lived near this mansion decades ago. Speaking of famous people, down the street is where three families and their famous patriarchs lived. Those men were Henry, Harvey and Thomas."

Erik says loudly, "Terrific!"

"They say," Miss Becky continues, "one or more of the men visited this mansion to attend parties. The era, or its fixed point in time history says, was called the Roaring Twenties."

Allie says and asks, "Just think, we're shooting on an historical location that was built almost a century ago. If in 1920 that era was called the Roaring Twenties, then I wonder what name the first decade of 2020 is called?"

Miss Becky and Erik agree how it is something to ponder. Boxes are stacked by the three of us. Erik excuses himself. He has to ready for shooting the next scene.

Miss Becky smiles saying, "Allie, we can work while discussing your family at the same time. Your mom told me that your great grandma's husband met Thomas, the inventor."

Allie, "Yes, he did!"

Miss Becky hangs up more clothes. Prana and Ivy are at the makeup station. With Prana's makeup done Miss Becky helps her dress for the next scene. Miss Becky picks out jewelry for Prana, and she thinks more about the famous inventor.

"I like hearing about history." Miss Becky continues, "The inventor lived nearby, and he was in his 80s when your grandpa was only seven."

Allie shares, "Young Ellis, known to my mom as Gramps, played in the backyards of Thomas and Henry only a few streets from here. Ellis rowed down the river with his brother Archie. They used a small boat they patched up after finding it in a trash heap."

Miss Becky, "Wow!"

Allie continues, "Both these men were neighbors, so it was easy to 'dock' off one's yard and play in both. Ellis and Archie climbed coconut palms in the yards knocking and cutting coconuts down. They would put them in their boat to carry and sell. The cost of a coconut with husk was 50 cents. Without the husk the boys got $5.00, but that only happened once."

"That's clever," says Miss Becky.

"Later," Allie says, "Gramps realized stealing coconuts was wrong. His mother was raising five children on her own, so the brothers did what they could to help. They ran around town barefoot, saving their shoes for school. In the 1930s, for them shoes were a luxury."

Miss Becky helps Prana and continues to listen. Prana listens too.

Miss Becky asks, "The brothers played in the inventor's lab, right?"

Allie answers, "Yes, that is until they got caught. With his cane, Thomas chased the boys out. It was not their fault. Back then, the lab had no security. Besides, it contained dangerous chemicals. Being young they didn't know better."

Miss Becky asks another question, "What did Ellis do when he grew up?"

"About 20 years later," Allie responds, "Gramps became a policeman, and one of his jobs was escorting celebrities. In the mid-1950s Gramps escorted a young singer. The famous man, like many rock and roll musicians in that era, didn't know he was making history!"

Miss Becky smiles saying, "Cool!"

Odds are she probably knows who the guitar playing musician was.

Allie continues, "More than once, Gramps escorted the musician to and from hotels and the places he performed. According to Gramps, the musician was very humble. My great grandfather called him a whipper snapper but not to his face. Gramps was just being Gramps."

"Wow again!" Miss Becky responds.

Allie's Movie Adventure

Great Grandparents
Ellis & Betty Jane

Below left, Ellis/Gramps age 7
when he "knew" Thomas

On right, Gramps as Police Major

Allie adds, "By the way, Gramps retired as a major on the police force having worked and served for 37 years."

Miss Becky says, "Now that's even more impressive."

It is closer now to shooting the first scene. Next is to find Deb... there she is!

Like Erik, Deb shares with others about the mansion's resident owner, Doreen Lehner. Deb tells us that she is retired with an historical and heroic background.

Our small group walks toward the interior front of the mansion. Erik tells us shooting will begin soon.

"For those who don't know," Deb says, "Doreen is a recipient of many medals. One is the Navy Marine Corps Medal for Heroism which the 35th President of the United States received."

"That's impressive." Allie says.

Deb adds, "He was the only presidential recipient of the same medal. Allie, do you know which president that was? That is okay, it will come to me later. Plus, Doreen Lehner was inducted into the Surface Navy Hall of Fame along with the 26th U.S. President, Theodore Roosevelt."

Deb finishes sharing about Doreen when the solarium door opens. There she is!

Doreen welcomes everyone and introduces herself. More crew members join the group. Doreen guides us through the middle of the estate to the front door. I ask her what she would like to be called. She says to call her Doreen, and she asks my name. After telling her, she turns to leave. She looks back speaking directly to me.

"Allie," says Doreen, "I'll be right back; I have to change. Miss Becky chose my dress. Ivy will check my makeup."

I tell her she is in good hands.

Erik is outside using the drone to shoot B-Roll footage. A future goal of mine is learning how to use a drone, but not on an active set. That is not the wisest thing to do. If so, CRASH could be the next sound everyone hears.

Christian tells Erik that Doreen is ready.

Doreen enters the ballroom at the front of the mansion wearing a gorgeous red gown. In a gown or blue jeans this lady has a commanding presence with a contagious smile.

The ballroom is a sight to behold. It is located between the front of the estate and the solarium. Every film would want to catch this ballroom, if not the mansion, on film. We are!

The two lead actors, Prana and Ivan, enter. The pets on set today are two dogs Genghis and Tater. They will be used in the background and are ready. Their wrangler is with them. Rehearsals and shooting begin.

Photo above by Navy corpsman comrade of Doreen Lehner

One of Doreen's medals here is the Navy Marine Corps Medal for Heroism. Her military title is Senior Chief, Hospital Corpsman, US Navy, Retired.

Doreen posing in her home/film location

Air conditioning is in Doreen's home. If it makes noise, though, it will be turned off during shooting. Even though modern electrical air conditioning was invented in 1902, it was not necessarily readily available. Of course, this estate did not use air conditioning in its early years.

My teacher says air conditioning is taken for granted. It was not practical until 1947-1960s, and then it was in the form of boxed window units. Businesses tended to use it readily first, but it was not common for new homeowners to use central air conditioning until the late 1960s.

Back on set, Doreen's lines are to include whatever she would say normally on an estate tour. No scripted lines today. Instead, we keep alert concerning continuity.

It being warm, Ivy keeps busy checking the three actors' makeup. Thanks Ivy!

By mid-afternoon Doreen is wrapped. She returns to her quarters and changes from gown to casual attire. Prana and Ivan head to Miss Becky to see what wardrobe they need for their next scene.

Doreen says, "Thank you for thinking of us. Thanks, too, for allowing me to be in the film. You enjoy the rest of the day. I am heading out to run errands. Make yourself at home!"

"You're welcome." Allie blurts out, "Oh, and his name is John F. Kennedy!"

Embarrassed, Allie says, "Sorry, the 35th president's name just popped into my head, but it didn't stay there."

Doreen and Deb laugh. They know why I blurted it out.

"Allie," Doreen says only to her, "Great job. Not many adults remember what JFK and I have in common. Thanks for that."

"You're welcome." Allie says to Doreen, "We want you to know that you'll be given the book that inspired this film. The author is Stevie Kinchen. Thanks for letting us use your home today."

Doreen smiles thanking us again and says she can hardly wait to see the book and film. We both agree to keep in touch.

The rest of the day progresses, and soon we wrap. All the shots went smoothly. Before we pack up, Erik, Heather, and Deb review the scenes' checklist. The production team confirms that it is a wrap at this location. Michayla and Christian pack up craft services making sure the kitchen is spotless. Heather and Ivy help.

We take photos in the mansion's ballroom, including a group selfie. We wish Doreen could be here for the group shot.

This completes a great day of shooting at the historical Mizner Estate. I am sure the film's cast and crew will agree that we experienced, and have become, part of the estate's history. Doreen Lehner made this possible.

Thank you, Doreen!

Chapter 16

That's a Wrap!

Summer's end is on the horizon, and that means filming is as well. Feeling right at home with my film family has been great, could not ask for better.

Everyone has been fun to work with. My parents visited on set to celebrate my birthday, and the film's cast and crew gave me a party. Of course, Erik took photos making more memories!

Miss Becky, Kristin, Rose, Heather, Ivy, and Prana all made the party possible. Rose said hiding the decorations and cake was the hardest part.

After the film wraps, post-production will begin. Edits, pickup shots, and stock footage are all part of post-production, and each is beneficial and necessary to filmmakers.

Erik says that one cannot have enough stock footage; he prefers not reusing shots very often. Cameramen constantly shoot extra images and video footage avoiding overuse. They store them digitally.

An additional part of post-production is its marketing. It is required in having a successful film and is sadly a waste of time, money, and energy when a film sits on the shelf.

A budget, and how it is used, can influence any film's future. Eventually films are promoted and released, and hopefully they result in large ticket sales and good reviews. Dad knows my concern. Besides, this kid cannot do very much to promote a film. He says Marlene and Erik have a handle on it!

One thing to never concern myself again is getting up for school. After rising most days at sunrise to get to the film set on time, getting up for school will be a cinch.

Back at home writing in my journal will be something to look forward to even though no one can read anything about the film yet. When Erik gives the okay, watch out! Who says my family can't read my journal now?!

Our film will be screened and part of film festivals. Dad says he will make sure we get to attend all the local screenings and film fests. Yay!

First things first though; editing can take as long as the shooting itself. As a result, there will not be Red Carpet events or viewings of our film until next year.

Patience in this business is essential. The cast and crew probably already have begun other projects. Like us, they will be contacted about our film's upcoming events.

Before next year's activities, and school this fall, we will visit family. We have a lot of family members and will visit as many as we can during the rest of the summer.

Family includes everyone from the Sunburst Convention, The Reel Awards, Uncle Jonathan, Aunt Emily, their children McKenzie, Kayleigh, Matthew, Audrey, and others. Some families live close by; others live farther away. Maybe some will travel here to see us.

Erik says, "Allie, there's another film I may be working on, and I'd like you to be part of it. Everyone from this film can work on it. Before saying 'no,' remember, there is such a thing as on-set tutors. Think about it!"

Chapter 17
"Ta for now"

After everyone signs my journal and script, selfies are taken. Erik takes group photos plus video footage. He says he will put them on social media when the time is right.

Taking Erik aside, I make sure he is aware of the future film he mentioned. The new project is all I think about.

Speaking for herself and family Allie says, "We accept!"

Erik grins. That means we will talk later.

He reminds everyone that it is time for the film's media management artist to do what she does best.

"Marlene Palumbo of Indienink Music," says Erik, "is aware of this film being wrapped. It is time now for her to get this film out there, and she will. She is good at what she does. I tell you this, as she may interview us. The two of us will be contacting you, and the interviews can happen over the phone."

Outside, everyone is loading. No sadness. We will most likely work together again real soon.

Heather, Marlene, and Erik will keep in touch. Erik will for sure, as he has pickup shots and vocals to complete.

Wardrobe supervisor Miss Becky reminds everyone to hold on to their set clothes until told otherwise. She suggests we label and store them properly, and she will email us updates.

Ivy suggests that we do not make any drastic changes to our bodies. Giggles fill the room.

Ivy says, "Seriously, don't change your hair color, its cut and style, no tattoos, piercings, or extreme tanning until you're cleared. If you have questions, contact me. I will email everyone too. Thanks."

Heather announces, "As a reminder, photography and video footage can be shot at other locations. Deb has a building that's used as a studio."

Deb says, "Allie, I see you thinking again."

Allie asks, "How did you come about having a studio?"

Deb responds, "You aren't the only one who asks that. Years after we built our home, we added a garage. Trying to think ahead, inside it we added an efficiency or small apartment. Later we converted the efficiency into a studio, and it has been useful as that ever since. It is still useful for overnight guests. In addition, it is a wonderful place for people to use for shooting film and television as well as for meetings, interviews, and castings. Everyone benefits using our studio."

Allie says, "That sounds great!"

Deb agrees and finishes packing. Not having much to pack she helps others. Just because the film is wrapped does not mean everyone is through working. Every single cable, light bulb, batteries, and of course cameras, sound equipment, craft services, and more, are loaded. Packing carefully helps protect and organize everything more easily as well.

Mom and Dad call. They are on the way.

Gram will check on things at her home for a while and then return to visit us. With no extra bed yet, Klara may stay in the den on the couch. All of us look forward to a full house!

When my parents took work-related trips, Gram cared for me. With her we would visit relatives, stay in their homes, and help work on their farms. It has been the reverse lately, as my family has been visiting me!

Gram has said, "Allie, doing more things on your own is all part of growing up. When we get together again it will mean even more."

Here, I am back to the reality of waiting for my folks. This former wardrobe station's window is a good place to see people come and go. The majority of crew are loaded up and ready to leave.

91

Stunt dogs, Jazzy (Sheepadoodle), Dolly (Havenese) and Baxter (Terrier), go outside with their handler to load up and leave. They are so obedient and quiet when on set. We don't play with them when they are working, as it might distract them.

Miss Becky will not leave until my parents arrive. Prana and Erik said the same. Ivy, Hadley, and Archer are nearby drawing and coloring on some of Ivy's sketches. Her art is so amazing it has been published in a book!

This adventure has been great, but it is not over. Making lasting friends and framily has been the best part!

Erik and Prana have more work ahead of them. They will continue to visit Dream Studios until Prana's vocals and music are wrapped. Prana and I recorded a song together last week. Erik has begun editing it. He is editing the film, other music and vocals as well.

The average moviegoer has no idea what goes into a film. After working on this project, I have come to appreciate the price of a movie ticket. It does not cost enough!

My window view reveals loaded vehicles, closed doors, and motors running. All are ready to leave. A car turns into the driveway.

Allie shouts, "Mom and Dad are here!"

Heather says, "Allie, your mom texted me saying they're going to wait in the car while we say our goodbyes."

Voices yell, "Allie!"

Turning around there's EVERYONE standing in one big group. The running cars outside must be empty.

Erik and Prana are in front. Miss Becky, Rose, Cassidy, Tay, Rob, Kevin, Ivan, Dr. Joe, and many others join them. The cast and crew must have snuck in not making a single peep.

"Okay everyone!" Erik yells, "You know the drill. Erik takes a video of us for the book's author Stevie Kinchen. We yell *Love Song and Power*!"

Everyone gathers closer, but the group seems to have grown. Newly here are Dunky, Rita, Anna, and Rusty. There is Mom and Dad! Jazzy, Dolly, and Baxter are here too!

Miss Becky brings the newcomers up front. Mom strains as she looks toward the door. Gram, Klara, and Splat enter!

Erik puts a chair up front and center for Gram. I sit on the floor with Splat. He puts his head on Gram's lap. Klara poses next to Mom and Dad. For the camera, first all of us smile, then we make funny faces yelling "framily!"

Miss Becky asks, "Allie, instead of saying goodbye, what do you say?"

Allie, "Ta for now, until my next adventure begins..."

Glossary

Acoustics - properties or qualities of a room or building that determine how sound is transmitted

Acting Resumé - a resume specially formatted for an actor who is seeking work/a role in film, TV, theater or another acting medium, it consists of an actor's stats/personal description, experiences and contact info usually of agent; these resumés are unique as combined with an actor's headshot fitting on a single, 8"x10" sheet of paper, either printed on back of headshot or attached to it

Actors (types) - main/principal, supporting, character, featured, and background. Character actor - a supporting actor who plays unusual, interesting, or eccentric characters, mostly used to describe television and film actors. The following is actor Miles Christian-Hart in the film *Love Song & Power* as "Tony Moon." In addition are two western characters portrayed by Miles and Prana Songbird.

B-Roll - any supplemental video considered to be secondary to primary or A-Roll footage; the extra footage captured to enrich the story you are telling and to have greater flexibility when editing

Call Sheet - a document sent out to the cast and crew of important details, including where they need to be for the following shoot day

Cell Dog - a rescue dog that is being housed with a prison inmate, with the goal of improving the lives of both

Clapper, clapboard, or Slate - main purpose to use this is to tell the post-production team when the camera has started and stopped recording; a device used in filmmaking and video production to assist in synchronizing of picture and sound plus designating and marking the various scenes and takes as they are filmed and audio-recorded.

Conchologists (shellers) - collection and study of mollusk shells, seashells with exoskeletons such as snails, clams, oysters... from oceans and freshwater

Photo: Kristin Mercedes Bence

Continuity - maintenance of continuous action and self-consistent detail in various scenes of a movie or broadcast

Drone - aerial cinematography shoots photographs or video from an aircraft or other flying object; is typically used for establishing shots, follow shots and action sequences in a film

Estate and Mansion - mansion and estate and be used interchangeably; difference is the size of the land of the property; an estate has extensive grounds

Feature Film - a feature-length film or a motion picture or movie with a minimum running time; such a film over 40 minutes to be eligible for an Academy Award; average is 75 to 210 minutes

Film Editing - editing that is both the creative and technical part of the post-production process of filmmaking

Film Release - authorization by owner of a completed film to a public exhibition of the film shown in theatres or for home viewing and is part of the marketing of the film for a wide or limited release

Film Score - original music written specifically to accompany film; can encompass an enormous variety of styles of music, depending on the nature of the films they accompany

Film Wardrobe - clothes worn by actors in films, plays, etc., the department that keeps and takes care of the clothes for films and plays by the wardrobe person or supervisor

Film Wrap - sometimes said to be an acronym for "Wind, Reel and Print" (WRAP)

Framily - a group of friends who are close like a family

Green Room - a lounge in a theater, broadcasting studio to use for resting and eating refreshments by performers when they are not onstage or on camera

Green Screen - a green background in front of which moving subjects are filmed allowing separately filmed backgrounds to be added to the final image

Gulf of Mexico - part of Atlantic Ocean bordered by the southeast coast of the United States and the east coast of Mexico

Headshot - a photograph of a person's, or animal's, head/face; headshots are in color, smiling, name on front, resumé on back

Me, Allie   Matt   Rose

Heyday – the period of one's greatest popularity, vigor, prosperity; earliest appearances in English were in the 16th century that expressed elation or wonder, similar to that of the English word hey, from which it derives; it comes from the old Germanic word "heida" meaning "hurrah!"

In the can - a film or piece of filming is in the can when it has been successfully completed; enjoying hot buttered popcorn while viewing the film later is always nice

Love - *Love Song & Power's* line producer Heather knows sign language, above is an image of it...
Sign Language - a system of communication using visual gestures and signs, as used by deaf people

Master Control Room - a broadcast operation common among most television stations and television networks; used for professional music and voice purposes

Media Room - a room in which the equipment or media for mass communication as telephone, fax, computer, etc. is fitted or used

Mentor - one who advises or trains

(The) Mizner Estate - historic manor house steeped in culture and elegance where Edison used to visit, history was made; designed by architect Addison Mizner

Mizner, Addison Cairns (1872-1933) - American resort architect who used the Mediterranean Revival and Spanish Colonial Revival styles in South Florida

Mucus is a noun; mucous is an adjective - The fluid that comes out of one's nose when congested is mucus, and the linings that secrete mucus are mucous membranes. Mucous comes from the Latin word "mucus" meaning snot, slime, mold...

"Mum's the word" - to keep silent or quiet; mum is a Middle English word (spoken after the Norman Conquest (from 1066-15th Century) meaning silent

Navy and Marine Corps Hall of Valor Medal - This award was established by an act of Congress on August 7, 1942. The decoration may be awarded to service members who, while serving in any capacity with the Navy or Marine Corps, distinguish themselves by heroism not involving actual conflict with an enemy.

Pandemic - epidemics occur worldwide over a very wide area, crossing international boundaries affecting large numbers of people

Pets on set – These are trained animals of any kind accompanied by a wrangler/trainer on movie and TV sets. They usually have their own headshot with resumé.

Portable Changing Room - a pop up changing room one can take anywhere that is freestanding and easily pops open

Recording Studio - specialized facility for sound recording, mixing, audio production of instrumental and voice

(The) Red Carpet - rolled at film festivals' award ceremonies celebrated as a special event with big lights, action & cameras

Reserves (in military) - a military organization composed of citizen-soldiers of a country who combine a military role or career with a civilian career; main role is to be available to fight when their military requires additional manpower.

Rookie Policeman - New police officers have a steep learning curve and typically are partnered with an experienced officer for at least the first month or two on the job. Police officers are considered a rookie for their first year on the job.

The Screen Actors Guild - American Federation of Television and Radio Artists (SAG-AFTRA) is an American labor union representing film & television actors, journalists, radio personalities, recording artists, singers, voice actors & other media professionals worldwide.

Solarium - a type of sunroom addition made entirely of glass with the purpose to trap sunlight allowing for an outdoor feel without having to go outside

Stunt performers (human & otherwise) – work in entertainment performing stunts in place of actors, like in fight scenes, car chases, motorcycle riding, vehicle chases and crashes, and other stunts. Examples: Prana and Miles on motorcycles and Jazzy

Klara & Allie's International Cooking Network

(inspired by & from
Cora's Cooking Network)

Royal Mashed Potatoes

Begin with fresh ingredients!

These creamy and delicious potatoes are a great add-on to Christmas dinner or just a snack on a cold night. Once you make it, it will become a family favorite.

Time is around 40 minutes and serves 10

6-7 large potatoes
6 T butter
7 T sour cream
1/2 cup of milk (add more depending on creaminess need)
1/2 t rosemary

First, peel the potatoes. Boil them until soft in a pot with the water about an inch above them. Then mash them in a large bowl. Add the sour cream, butter (option is to melt it first), milk and rosemary. Mix well and serve hot. Tip: I find electric mixers work best for creaminess. Enjoy!

Chunky Choco Chip Cookies with Oats

This recipe is our dream cookie with just enough coconut to give it that summery, fresh, tropical taste but not too much making them dry and grainy. We add lots of chocolate and oats to make them thick and dense, so they break off easily. It makes about two dozen cookies and takes 30 minutes.
Have fun (baking)!

1 cup plus 12 tablespoons softened butter
1 1/2 cups firmly packed brown sugar
1 cup white sugar
4 eggs
2 teaspoons vanilla
3 cups flour
2 tsp baking soda
2 tsp ground cinnamon
dash of nutmeg (optional)
1 teaspoon salt
6 cups oats
2 cups of semi-sweet chocolate chips
1 cup dark chocolate chip
1 cup coconut

Instructions:
1. Heat oven to 350 Fahrenheit. In a large bowl mix the butter and sugars until creamy.
2. Add the eggs and vanilla, beat well.
3. In a medium bowl sift the flour, baking soda, salt, nutmeg and cinnamon. Slowly add it to the wet.
4. Add the oats, chocolate, and coconut, then mix well and place on a pan in 3-inch diameter balls. Cook for 8-10 minutes till crispy and brown, cool and enjoy!

Made in the USA
Columbia, SC
20 April 2021